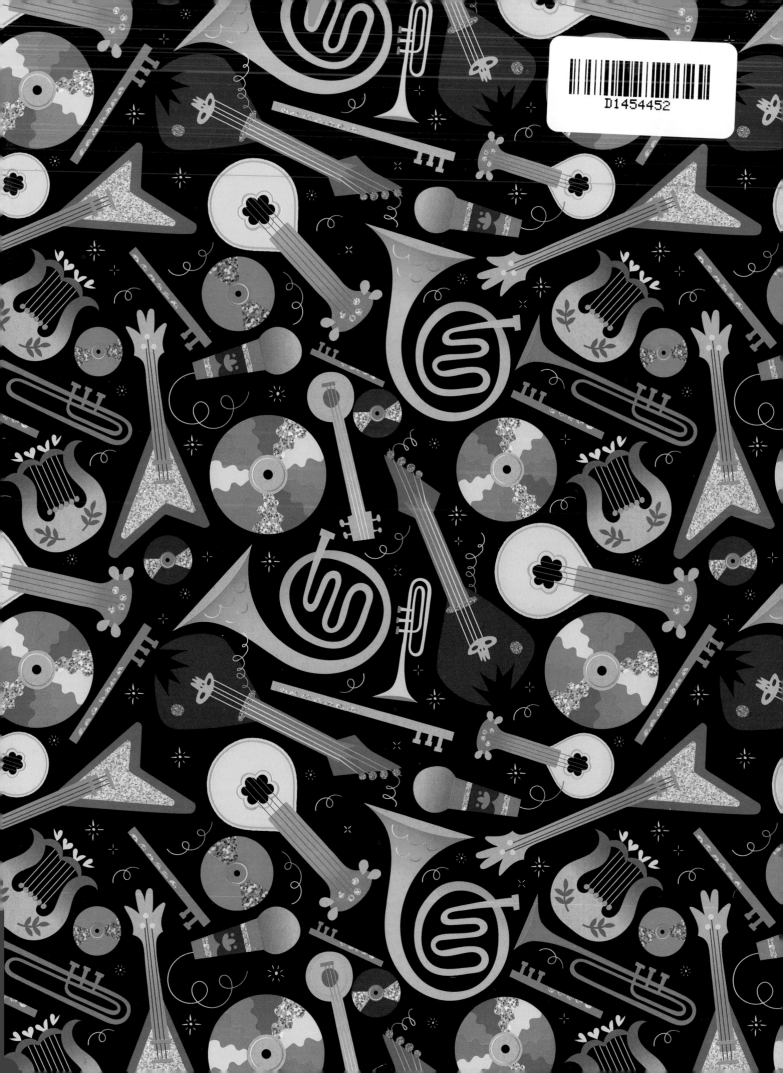

Queen Poppy

Branch

Biggie and Mr. Dinkles

Guy Diamond

Tiny Diamond

Satin and Chenille

Fuzzbert

Smidge

King Peppy

Cloud Guy

Cooper

Sheila B.

King Trollex

Techno Troll

Techno Troll

Trollzart

A Cherub and Pennywhistle

Delta Dawn

Hickory

King Quincy

Queen Essence

Prince D

Queen Barb

Debbie

Riff

EGMONT
We bring stories to life

First published in Great Britain in 2020
by Egmont Books UK Ltd
2 Minster Court, 10th floor, London EC3R 7BB
www.egmontbooks.co.uk

Designed by Claire Yeo
Written/edited by Lauren Holowaty

This book is an original creation by Egmont UK Limited

Parental guidance is advised for all craft and colouring activities. Always ask an adult to help
when using glue, paint and scissors. Wear protective clothing and cover surfaces to avoid staining.

Stay safe online. Egmont is not responsible for content hosted by third parties.

Egmont takes its responsibility to the planet and its inhabitants very seriously.
We aim to use papers from well-managed forests run by responsible suppliers.

ISBN 978 1 4052 97318
70903/002
Printed in Italy

DREAMWORKS Trolls

This Troll-tastic Annual belongs to

Rebecca

Contents

Annual 2021

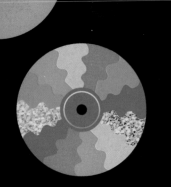

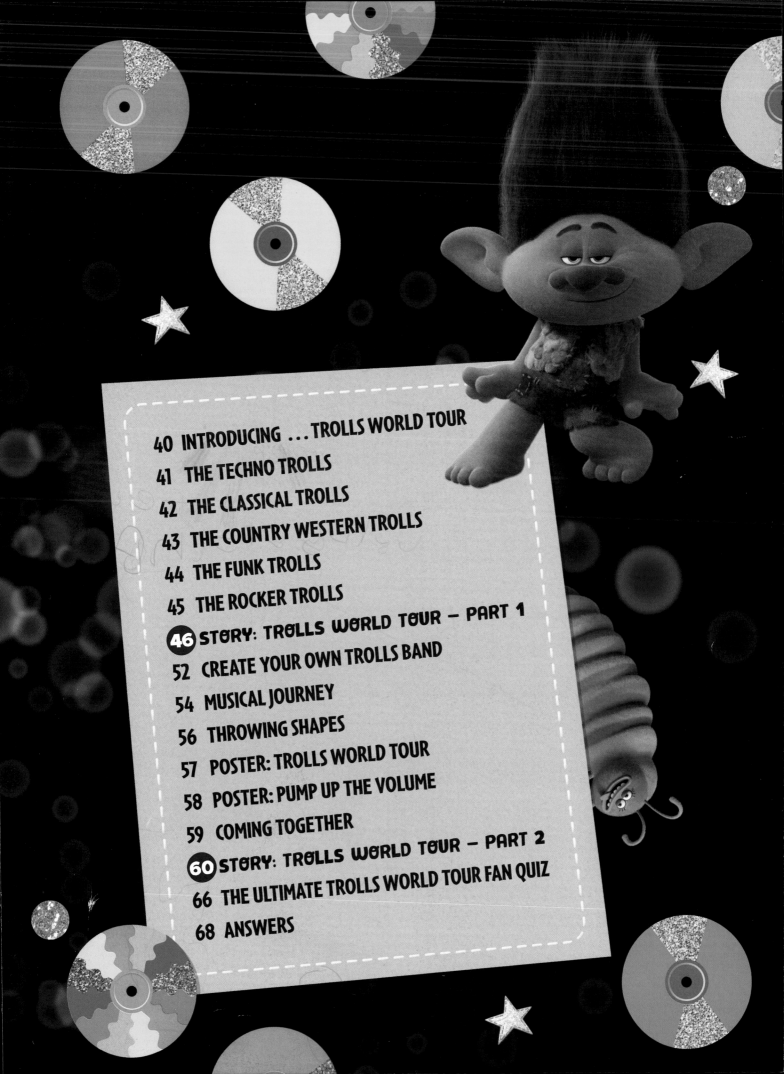

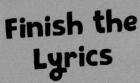

Introducing ...

Queen Poppy

Super-positive **Poppy** is the leader of the Trolls and everyone's loveable hero. She believes that with a song in your heart you can do anything, and tries to get everyone else to think the same. She loves singing about everything in life. Well, why say it, when you can sing it?

Finish the Lyrics

Try making up your own song lyrics, just like Poppy. Add some words to finish these lines. There are no right or wrong answers, just have fun!

Life is full of _silly_

....

that make me smile.

Sometimes when I _poop_

I like to sit for a while.

But when I hear a beat, I jump to my _feet_,

And _LOLUGETSLNG_

until it's time to sleep!

Branch

Branch spends a lot of his time wondering if he's the only sane one in a town full of constantly happy and excitable Trolls. He's always ready and waiting for things to go wrong!

Match the Moves

Look carefully at these shadows. Which one is an exact match of Branch dancing?

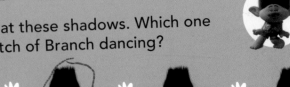

a b c d

Biggie and Mr. Dinkles

Biggie is a huge softie with a great big heart. He's very emotional and often bursts into tears when things are a bit sad or even if they're happy! He carries his pet, **Mr. Dinkles**, everywhere he goes and has been known to dress him up in cute little outfits!

Where's Mr. Dinkles?

Oh no, Biggie can't find his precious Mr. Dinkles. Quickly, follow the lines to find out which way he should go, before he bursts into tears!

a

b

c

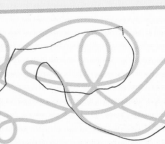

Answers on pages 68–69

Guy Diamond and Tiny Diamond

Rap it up!

Help Tiny Diamond finish the rap below by using the words to fill in the gaps.

Covered from sparkly top to glistening toe in glitter, **Guy Diamond** has a super shiny, super confident personality! He is full of energy and knows how to party! His son, **Tiny Diamond**, is a small Troll with a huge talent for hip-hop and rapping!

feet

beat

fun

friends

My name is ͭᶦⁿʸ Diamond

And I glitter in the sun

I hang out with Troll friends

And we have so much fun!

I love to sway to the hip-hop beat

I dance and move and tap my feet!

Tiny Diamond

sun

Introducing ...

Cooper

This happy and enthusiastic Troll is always ready to charge the dance floor with his funky moves. And he's about to discover just where those funky moves came from!

Colour by Numbers

Use the number key to help you colour in the picture of Cooper.

Colour Key

1 = light blue
2 = red
3 = pink
4 = green
5 = dark blue

King Peppy

This brave leader of the Trolls is a bit of a Troll legend. He always has a wise word and knows how to keep happiness in Trolls Village.

Escape from Bergen Town

Help King Peppy show the Trolls the way from Bergen Town to Trolls Village by guiding him through this maze.

Answers on pages 68–69

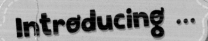

Introducing ...

Prince D

This four-legged prince is the son of King Quincy and Queen Essence. Ever since he was a young prince, he's felt like he's been missing a vital part of himself, but he's not sure why ... until he meets his long-lost twin brother, Cooper!

Smidge

She may look teeny-tiny, but this Troll has a whole lotta voice and it's surprisingly deep and low. She loves keeping herself busy with lots of very different hobbies.

Hobby Search

Can you find some of Smidge's surprising hobbies in the grid? Words may read from side to side or up and down, but not diagonally.

C	A	Y	T	C	H	D	W	A	C
G	L	T	S	O	G	B	E	E	M
C	R	O	C	H	E	T	I	N	G
R	F	E	M	G	P	W	G	A	N
E	O	B	G	C	A	A	H	Q	I
N	C	P	F	B	D	Y	T	C	G
A	U	C	Y	F	C	A	L	W	N
G	I	V	H	C	D	E	I	A	I
T	K	F	N	P	B	L	F	V	S
H	E	A	V	Y	M	E	T	A	L
M	U	G	R	I	S	K	I	B	D
B	C	T	A	A	O	A	N	D	A
D	R	D	H	R	I	F	G	C	A

CROCHETING

HEAVY METAL

WEIGHTLIFTING

SINGING

Answers on pages 68–69

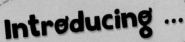

Satin and Chenille

Stylish twins **Satin** and **Chenille** know everything there is to know about fashion, from luxurious haute couture to the latest high street trends.

Copy Colouring!

Look at the picture to help you colour in Satin and Chenille. Make sure their outfits look divine!

Cloud Guy

Always mysterious and sometimes mischievous, **Cloud Guy** loves high-fives and wants to have fun. He's also super-cool and always willing to help out.

Whirling Word Wheel

Circle every fourth letter in this whirling cloud to discover the name of the Troll who Cloud Guy likes to tease.

→ C P O B Y
N C X T
M I H
N B
O P
M R
S
N A
I G
T A
D G A S R P

Sheila B.

This is Poppy's extra-special flower balloon ready to help the Pop Troll queen, Branch and the rest of the Trolls on their journeys. Sheila B. is the perfect way to travel in bunches of style!

Spot the Difference

a   **b**

Take a look at these two pictures of Sheila B. Can you spot five differences between them?

Answers on pages 68-69

Fuzzy Reflection

Draw Fuzzbert's reflection in the mirror. Did you know his nickname is Twinkle Toes and he just loves tickling his friends?

Fuzzbert

Made almost entirely of bright green Troll hair, **Fuzzbert** communicates by making deep noises in his throat, but amazingly everyone understands him!

History

Once upon a time the unhappy Bergens discovered the super-happy and super-tasty Trolls. They kept them captive to eat on Trollstice ...

... but one year, the Trolls escaped before the Bergens' Chef could serve them up for Prince Gristle's first Trollstice feast. Chef is banished from Bergen Town for letting them escape.

"No Troll left behind!"

Twenty years pass and Poppy becomes the leader of the Trolls. The Trolls celebrate with an extra-loud party for her coronation.

The former Bergan Royal Chef overhears the party. Finally, she can get her revenge! She captures some of the Trolls.

Poppy goes to rescue her friends. Branch refuses to help, so Poppy sets out on her own.

Branch changes his mind and catches up with Poppy just in time to save her from a terrible fate. Optimistic Poppy sings all the way to Bergen Town.

"Oh my gah!"

The Trolls befriend Bridget, a shy Bergen scullery maid, and discover she's in love with King Gristle!

The Trolls offer to help Bridget catch the eye of the King. Lady Glittersparkles is born!

To save himself, a Troll called Creek betrays the other Trolls and helps Chef capture the rest of the Trolls. Poppy loses hope and her colour fades away.

Branch sings to Poppy, restoring her positivity and her colours.

Bridget frees the Trolls. Poppy worries what will happen to her new Bergen friend and turns back to help her.

"Nobody left behind!"

"Hooray!"

The Bergens learn that happiness is found within, not from eating Trolls. King Peppy passed the Torch of Freedom to Poppy, and she is finally crowned Queen of the Trolls.

Poppy's Flower Code

Trolls love puzzles. Sometimes Poppy uses a colourful flower code when she wants to say something to her friends. It does sound like a fun way to communicate!

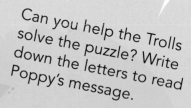

Can you help the Trolls solve the puzzle? Write down the letters to read Poppy's message.

Who's That?

Hurry! The Bergens are coming!
The Trolls are running for cover –
they hope Chef doesn't spot them.

Do you recognise the Trolls in these close-up pictures? Write their names in the frames.

Let's make:

Dance Move Cube

Ask an adult to help make this cool dance cube so you can play a fun dance game with your friends!

How to do it:

1 Carefully cut out the shape along the dashed lines.

2 Fold along the yellow dotted lines.

3 Glue the grey tabs together. Once dry, you're ready to play!

You'll need:
- Scissors
- Glue

How to play?

Put on your favourite music, then take it in turns to roll the dance cube and perform each dance move!

Your Cube

Slide to the side, then slide back again.

©DWA LLC

Play air guitar.

Point one arm up to the sky then down across your body.

Jump your legs out to the side, reach down, touch the floor and stretch up.

Do the snake by weaving your arms up and down.

Swing your whole body from side to side.

Hug the Bug

The Trolls are looking for bugs. The forest is full of strange and beautiful creatures. Can you help the Trolls find all of them?

How many bugs of each type can you see in the picture? Count them and write the totals on the lines.

Answers on pages 68-69

TROLLS
WHOSE JUICE?

Sript adaptation by: Maciej Nowak-Kreyer

SMIDGE WAS DREAMING ...

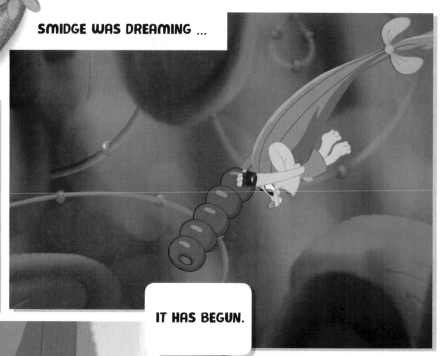

IT HAS BEGUN.

SMIDGE WAS READY TO SELL HER STOUTBERRY JUICE.

PLEASE, DON'T FREAK OUT WHEN I SAY THIS BUT ... SMIDGE'S STOUTBERRY JUICE IS AVAILABLE AT THE MARKET!

NO NEED TO PUSH, MAMA SMIDGE HAS PLENTY TO GO ROUND.

THANKS SMIDGE! YOUR JUICE IS SO GOOD, IT'S THE ONLY THING CHENILLE AND I AGREE ON.

NO! THIS IS THE ONLY THING CHENILLE AND I DON'T DISAGREE ON!

SUDDENLY ...

GUY DIAMOND PROUDLY PRESENTS THE TASTE SENSATION ...

GLITTERADE!

JUICE AND GLITTER? IT'S TRES CHIC.

I WANT TO DISAGREE BUT I CAN'T. TRES CHIC INDEED.

MEANWHILE SMIDGE WAS NOT IMPRESSED.

SPLASH!

SMIDGE I WASN'T TRYING TO TAKE YOUR THING.

I JUST WANTED TO SAY HOW SORRY I AM ABOUT YOUR JUICE STAND. IT'S TOO BAD YOU HAVE TO SHUT IT DOWN. STOUTBERRY JUICE IS MY THING, SILLY.

25

SHUT IT DOWN OR I'LL SHUT IT DOWN FOR YOU.

LOOK, SMIDGE, I GOT INTO THE JUICE GAME 'CAUSE IT LOOKED FUN AND FRANKLY I LIKE THE ATTENTION. AND I'M NOT LEAVING JUST 'CAUSE YOU SAY SO.

IT'S HUG TIME!

NEXT MORNING ...

GLITTERADE OPEN FOR BUSINESS! GUY DIAMOND PRESENTS HIS BRAND-NEW TASTE SENSATION ...

OR, GET A BERRY JUICE. THIS WAY!

Y'KNOW I THOUGHT I WANTED GLITTERADE, BUT THAT SIGN HAS SOME CRAZY POWER OVER ME.

Fashion Fun

Accessories are just as important as the clothes themselves. Satin and Chenille design amazing jewellery that goes with any outfit.

Work out the pattern and finish the bracelets.

1

2

3

Say Cheese!

Look at this awesome snapshot! It is Poppy's favourite photo with her friends. Unfortunately she dropped it and it broke into many pieces!

Help Poppy repair the photo by matching the pieces to the right places in the frame.

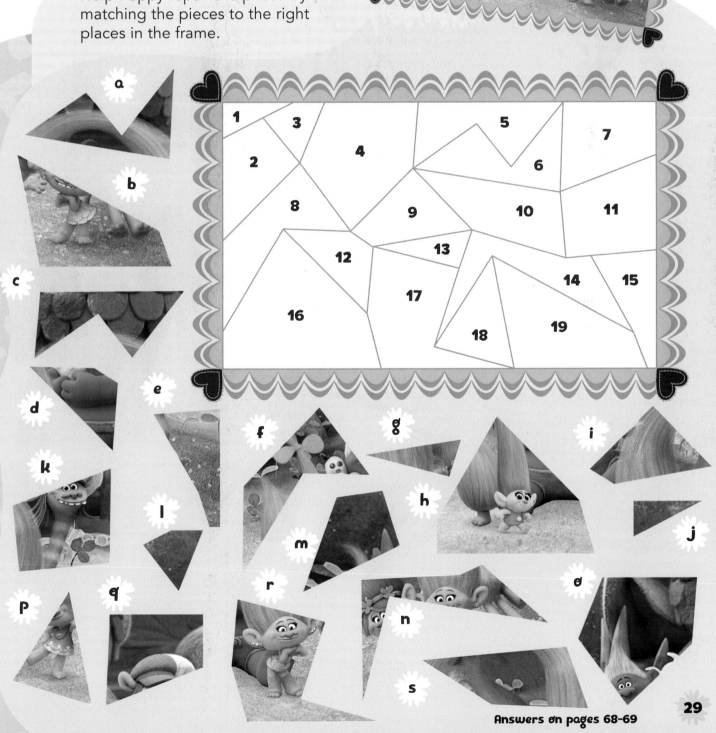

Answers on pages 68-69

Draw Your Troll

Follow the instructions below to draw your own Troll. Remember to fill in the blanks in the words to find out what colours you should use.

1 Your Troll has **o_ange** skin. His nose is **_reen** and his eyes are **bro_n.** There are glitter freckles on his cheeks and he is always smiling.

2 He has **_ed** curly hair and wears a **b_ue** hair band.

3 He wears **g_ey** trousers and walks around barefoot.

4 He is holding a **p_nk** cupcake in one hand and an **y_llo_** ice cream in the other.

5 He wears a **p_rple** shirt with four **bl_ck** buttons and there is a small ice cream stain on the sleeve.

6 He's walking in the Trolls' **gree_** forest, enjoying the nice weather.

memory Game

Look carefully at the picture for approximately three minutes, then turn over to answer the challenging questions about it.

Question Time!

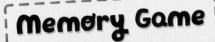

Question Time!

1 Who is standing at the front in the middle?

2 What is Poppy holding in her hand?

3 Where is Mr. Dinkles?

4 What is Fuzzbert holding up in the air?

5 What colour is Cooper's hat?

6 What colour is King Peppy's microphone?

7 Who is the tallest?

8 What shape are Branch's glasses?

9 What colour is the bow in Smidge's hair?

10 How many Trolls are in the picture?

If you answered all the questions correctly you are **Troll-tastic!**

If you answered half the questions you need to work on your concentration skills.

If you answered less than five questions turn back and try again!

Answers on pages 68-69

Dot-to-Dot

Join the dots to find out what these Trolls are waiting to eat!

33

Part 2

THAT'S RIGHT, IT'S YOUR FRIENDLY NEIGHBOURHOOD BERRY JUICE BUG! NOW THE JUICE COMES TO YOU!

SMIDGE IS WORKING SO HARD TO SELL HER JUICE THAT SHE HAS SET UP A DELIVERY COMPANY!

THEN GUY TAKES THINGS EVEN FURTHER ...

GLITTERADE FROM THE SKY!

MY BAD. KIND OF HARD TO STEER.

CRASH!

THAT'S IT. NO MORE MRS. NICE SMIDGE. THIS IS A JOB FOR ...

SMIDGE HAS COME UP WITH A PLAN ...

SUDDENLY!

ATTENTION TROLLS! THE GROWLS WE HEARD RECENTLY WERE GROWLBEASTS! SO PLEASE, NO TROLL SHOULD GO NEAR MISTY MEADOWS FOR ANY REASON!

MISTY MEADOWS! OHMYGUH OHMYGUH OHMYGUH!

MISTY MEADOWS ...

ZOOM!

GUY, YOU GOTTA GET OUT OF HERE! GROWLBEASTS ARE HEADED THIS WAY.

HA! YOU REALLY THINK I'M THAT DUMB. SORRY, BUT I HAVE IT ON AUTHORITY OF A HELPFUL STRANGER ...

OMG! THAT WAS YOU ... YOU LIED ... ABOUT VIPS? IS NOTHING SACRED?

SORRY, GUY! IT'S REALLY DANGEROUS!

SO WHAT? I'D RATHER FACE AN ENTIRE HERD OF GROWLBEASTS THAN SPEND A MINUTE WITH YOU, SMIDGE ...

NOPE! WRONG! I WAS WRONG!

SUDDENLY!

36

37

It's a Troll's Life

It's time to really experience the Troll way of life. Read on to find out more!

1

Hug Time

Drop everything, it's Hug Time! Trolls love to hug. When their special Hug Time watches chime, they grab those nearest and pull them into an epic group hug. The more Trolls the merrier!

2

Hair

Troll hair is super-strong and the Trolls can stretch and shape their hair instantly into any form you can imagine! Trolls can swing and zip-line through trees by their hair or even snooze in Troll-hair hammocks – the possibilities are endless!

3

Crafting

The amazingly creative Trolls love to express themselves by crafting, using fun colours and textures to make art, outfits, scrapbooks and lots of other new things!

4

Critters

Trolls Village is home to lots of friendly and huggable critters. From Biggie's pet, Mr. Dinkles, to the Caterbus! They create tasty treats, form sweet harmonies and help Trolls zoom around the village.

5

Music

Trolls Village is constantly pulsing with music and it's not unusual for a single song to start off an impromptu all-day dance party! Music is a very important element of every Troll's lifestyle and opportunities to express themselves in song and dance are never passed up. As Poppy says: "With a song in your heart, anything is possible!"

The Pop Trolls

Until recently **Poppy** and her friends thought they were the only Trolls in the world, but they're about to find out there are all sorts of other Trolls too! Techno Trolls, Classical Trolls, Country Western Trolls, Funk Trolls, Rocker Trolls ...

In fact, **King Peppy**, Poppy's father explains to her that she, Branch and their friends are all actually ... **Pop Trolls!**

Pop's Missing?

Take a close look at the picture of the Pop Trolls below. Then cover it up and try to draw all the missing parts in the picture. Don't forget to colour in the picture when you've finished.

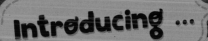

The Techno Trolls

Down in the dark ocean depths is the kingdom of the Techno Trolls, whose shimmering mermaid tails are swishing, as their hearts pound in unison to the *thoompa, thoompa* beats!

King Trollex

The Techno Trolls

The energetic **Techno Trolls** love all forms of electronic dance music. They're extremely enthusiastic and are the greatest fans of techno, dub step and the underwater rave scene. They know how to enjoy a good dance party!

Constantly upbeat and confident, **King Trollex** is the incredibly kind leader of the Techno Trolls. He makes sure that they stay true to their values of peace, love and harmony and their hearts all beat in sync.

Techno Reef Maze

Help the Techno Trolls dance their way through the LED-lit digital dance maze to their leader, King Trollex.

The Classical Trolls

Please be upstanding for this elegant ensemble from Symphonyville – the cherubs, Pennywhistle and their amazing conductor ... Trollzart!

The leader of the Classical Trolls, **Trollzart**, certainly looks composed. But when his precious golden string is threatened, the baton-wielding virtuoso will defend classical music until the very last note!

The cherubs all use their angelic gossamer wings to float around Symphonyville in perfect time and harmony.

Pennywhistle might seem like a timid, tiny tin whistle at first, but she always knows how to make herself heard.

Sudoku Symphony!

Help Trollzart keep his orchestra in order by completing this classic grid. Each instrument should only appear once in each row, column and 3x2 rectangle box enclosed in a bold line.

Answers on pages 68-69

The Country Western Trolls

Yee-haw! How y'all doing? Mayor Delta Dawn and her Country Western Trolls, hail from the middle of Troll heartland itself, Lonesome Flats. Being half-horse and half-Troll, these folks sure know how to two-step (or four-step!) waltz!

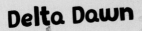

Delta Dawn

Hickory

There's something mysterious about this smooth-singing, ruggedly handsome Country Western Troll, who's ready and waiting to swoop into town and save the day.

The fearless leader of the Country Western Trolls, **Mayor Delta Dawn**, is tasked with keeping the peace in Lonesome Flats. She's super-smart, sassy and has a beautiful singing voice. She'll do anything to protect her town and what lies at its heart – country music!

Line Dance Line-Up

Join in the country music line dancing fun by looking at the patterns and working out who comes next in each line. Heel, toe, and off you go!

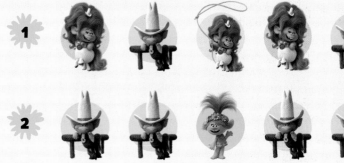

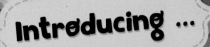

Introducing ...

The Funk Trolls

Vibe City is a gigantic flying saucer, floating high above Trolls Kingdom ... The super-sparkly and ever-so-shiny spaceship is made entirely from platinum records and is home to the truly spectacular Funk Trolls.

King Quincy and Queen Essence

The royal leaders of the Funk Trolls are **King Quincy** and **Queen Essence**. The majestic pair share their royal duties while presiding over their funky flying kingdom and looking for their long-lost son.

Get Funky!

It's time to bust some crazy moves with Prince D and the Funk Trolls!

Slide across the grid from the start to the finish by following this sequence:

 1 2 3

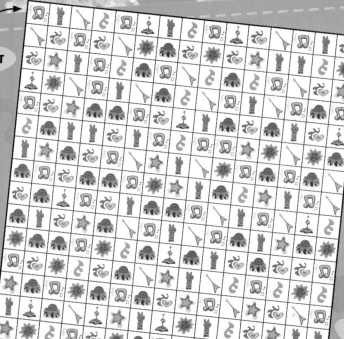

START

FINISH

Answers on pages 68–69

The Rocker Trolls

Queen Barb and her army of Rocker Trolls think nothing but rock music rocks, and that it is time everyone in Trolls Kingdom realised that too!

Debbie

Queen Barb

Barb's pet bat, **Debbie**, is totally adorable ...if you like your pets snarling and with huge teeth that is! Debbie delivers invitations from Barb to the other Trolls tribes.

Fierce-looking **Barb** is fed up of rock music constantly playing second fiddle to pop. She can't stand pop music and it's upbeat melodies and catchy rhymes that get stuck in your head, get stuck in your head, get stuck ... Enough is enough! The time has come for a "hard rock apocalypse" where she will have the power to control ... all music!

Riff

The Rocker Trolls all believe in rock domination and die-hard rocker **Riff** is no exception. He will do whatever it takes to please Barb. If she says, "Rock!" he says, "How hard?"

Who Rocks?

Spot all the different parts of the Rocker Trolls in the picture before they try to take over the kingdom!

Story: Trolls World Tour

Poppy and Branch were about to find out that their world was a whole lot bigger than they thought. That there were in fact lots of other Trolls they had never even heard of and entire new lands outside of Trolls Village! Including the watery world of the Techno Trolls, down in the hidden depths of the ocean ...

"Let's do it again!" called King Trollex. He was pumping out a thumping dance song as he swam around his royal DJ booth. A huge crowd of Techno Trolls and their families were dancing along to the King's beats.

"Tonight is about family, love and music," announced the King. **"Now, get ready for the drop ... wait for it ... wait for it ..."**

The Techno Trolls were going wild waiting for the beat to continue ...

BOOM!

The beat finally dropped, and the crowd jumped and swayed to the beat in unison.

But in the distance a big dark creature was swimming towards them, menacingly ...

The machine-like creature approaching had a sign on it saying, **ROCK TOUR**. The King didn't know yet, but it was the Rocker Trolls' tour bus. Just then it's mouth opened to reveal ... **Queen Barb** – the queen of the Rocker Trolls.

King Trollex turned the music off and reassured the crowd. **"Don't worry, we'll get back to the party in a minute,"** he said. **"Let me just take care of this real quick."**

Queen Barb introduced herself to King Trollex and said, **"I'm throwing the biggest party the world has ever seen, and ... I'm going to need your string, bro."**

"No way," said King Trollex. **"If we lose our string, we lose our music."**

"Beep-beep-beep bwoop isn't music!" cried the Rocker Queen. **"Real music is rock music!"**

Queen Barb explained her plan to take over Trolls Kingdom with her music – rock music! She and her rock army were going to make everyone play nothing but rock!

"NOW, WHO'S READY TO ROCK?"

... shouted Queen Barb at the top of her voice.

The next morning, in the land of the Pop Trolls, Queen Poppy leapt out of bed ready to start the day. She raced outside to sing and dance with her friends to a happy pop tune all about having fun!

Meanwhile, Branch was hanging out in his underground bunker staring at a picture of him and Poppy. He wanted to tell her how much he really liked her, but it was just so hard to find the right time and the courage to say it. Maybe he'd get a change to tell her at the morning's dance?

Branch zip-lined into the village, ending up right by Poppy's side for the morning's song and dance. He was just about to speak to the Queen when they heard Guy Diamond shouting, **"Poppy, come quick! It's an EMERGENCY!"**

Poppy and Branch raced off to find him.

"What's wrong, Guy?" asked Poppy.

"I'm having ..." cried Guy,

"... a BABY!"

Suddenly there was a **POP!** A little egg burst out of Guy's hair and cracked open mid-air! Out came a tiny glitter Troll who looked just like Guy!

"Awwww," everyone cooed looking at the super-cute little guy.

Guy Diamond was so happy. **"What should I name him?"** he asked.

"How about ... Tiny Diamond?" suggested Poppy.

Everyone was very surprised when Tiny Diamond jumped up, put on some cool shades and started to rap in a deep voice!

"Welcome to the family, little buddy," Poppy said to Tiny Diamond.

"Thanks, Aunt Poppy!" said Tiny Diamond. **"And thanks to this silver-haired daddy of mine for bringing me into this world."**

The Trolls sang and danced together to celebrate the wonderful new arrival.

"Peace and love!" called Tiny when the dance was over. **"Bless up. Tiny and Daddy out."**

"OK, bye!" Poppy called to them, as they walked off home.

After everyone had left, Poppy and Branch tried to do a high-five, but they just kept missing. Branch felt sad, if they couldn't even make a good high-five connection, how would they ever be more than friends? But his thoughts were interrupted by a loud scream,

AHHHHHHHH!

"What was that?" thought Poppy and Branch. They ran towards the scream.

It was Biggie. **"Help! I'm being harangued by a monster!"** A bat-like creature with red eyes and long teeth was flying around his head.

Poppy grabbed the creature, but it got stuck in her hair.

Branch zoomed over, pulled it out, and calmed it down with some shushing. **"There you go. Who's a good boy?"** The creature started to purr!

Everyone was a bit scared until ...

"Don't worry, everyone," said Queen Poppy, finding a letter attached to the creature. **"It looks like it's brought an invitation."**

"Ohhh," said Cooper. **"That's a relief."**

Poppy read the letter out loud ...

To Queen Poppy,

Barb, Queen of Rock, announces her 'One Nation of Trolls Under Rock World Tour'. Bring your string to the biggest party the world has ever seen!

Poppy was confused. What did that mean? Were there other Trolls out there? She needed to ask her father, King Peppy.

"There are other kinds of Trolls," said King Peppy.

"That's great!" said Poppy.

"They aren't like us," said the king. **"They're different. We love music with an upbeat melody. That's pop music. That's what makes us Pop Trolls. These other Trolls sing and dance differently."**

She left in a huff and decided to come up with her own plan – she was going to meet Queen Barb! She found the bat creature, gave it a glittery makeover, and sent it to Queen Barb with an invitation.

Nearby, Sheila B., a big flower-faced balloon with a basket was waiting to carry Poppy off on her secret mission.

King Peppy suggested they break down into a smaller group. Then he led just Poppy and Branch to a grotto and showed them an ancient scroll ...

"Our world was once without song or dance," began the king. "Until someone made a **'TWANG'** sound plucking a hair from a Troll. Our ancestors were inspired, so they took six strings (Troll hairs) and those strings had the power to control all music! But then everyone argued about what music they wanted to hear. There was only one solution: each tribe took a string for their own music and went their separate ways."

"And now Barb wants to reunite the strings so the Trolls world can be one big party again," said Poppy.

"Won't having the strings together lead to fighting?" said Branch.

"Exactly," said King Peppy, as he showed them where the pop music string was. **"We must keep it safe and run from the Rocker Trolls."**

But Poppy disagreed, **"But we don't even know what we're running from."**

Branch guessed Poppy's plan. **"Wait! I'm coming with you!"**

Poppy was secretly pleased he was coming.

"Oh yeah," said Sheila B. **"Road trip! In the sky!"**

Find out what Poppy's secret mission is when the story continues on page 60!

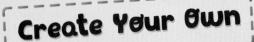

Create Your Own

Trolls Band

Get everyone singing and dancing together just like Queen Poppy wants to do, by designing your very own ultimate Trolls World Tour band!

1. Roll the dice.
2. The first number you roll is the first word in your band name.
3. The second number you roll is the second word in your band name.

List 1:
1. Troll-a-delic
2. All the
3. Musical
4. Symphonic
5. Troll-tastic
6. Different

List 2:
1. Stars
2. Beats
3. Heroes
4. Rainbows
5. Voices
6. Sprinkles

Tick the boxes:

The Trolls I'd love to have in my band are:

Poppy ☐

Branch ☐

Trollzart ☐

Delta Dawn ☐

King Trollex ☐

Queen Barb ☐

Riff ☐

Prince D ☐

Tiny Diamond ☐

My band name is ...

52

Design your stage outfits here!

The instruments my band uses are:

Tick the boxes:

The names of some of our epic songs are:

Your songs can be a mash-up of all sorts of different types of music!

Musical Journey

Head off on a Troll-tastic musical journey by playing this song and dance game! Will you be the one to join Poppy on stage at the finish? Roll the dice to find out!

How to play:

1 Roll the dice. Move your counter the right number of spaces and follow the instructions on the squares you land on.

2 The first player to join Poppy on stage is the winner!

You'll need:
- 1 dice
- Coins or other counters

9 **Dance Move!**
Can you floss? Attempt it now, then roll again!

10 **Make Some Noise!**

8

7

6 **Make Some Noise!**
Can you rap like Tiny Diamond? Try making up your own rap, then move on 2 spaces.

5

4 **Dance Move!**
Time to warm up for your dance routine. Do 5 star jumps, then move on 1 space.

3

2

1

START

31

30

29

28

27 **Dance Move!**
Stop to try out some new dance steps. Miss a go!

26

25
Pretend to play the drums in the air and make the sounds too! Move on 1 space.

11

12

Try yodelling, "Yo-de-lay-he-hoo!" 5 times, then move on one space.

13

Dance Move!

Jump up, wiggle your hips for 10 seconds, then sit down. Wiggle on 2 spaces.

14

Make Some Noise!

Stop to sing some lyrics of your favourite song. Miss a go!

32

33

Make Some Noise!

Sing your favourite song as loudly as you can. If another player guesses what it is, move on 1 space!

34

15

37

36

What's your favourite dance move? Do it now and move on 2 spaces.

Dance Move!

35

16

17

Dance Move!

Jump up and slide to the side, then slide on to the next space!

38

You made it to the stage!

FINISH

39

44

18

40

Make Some Noise!

Can you hum a tune while dancing? If yes, dance on one space!

Make Some Noise!

Poppy calls a final singing rehearsal. Miss a go!

Sing with Poppy, then take a bow!

19

43

Dance Move!

Poppy calls a last minute dance routine rehearsal. Miss a go!

41

42

20

24

Dance Move!

Put 4 dance moves together, then teach your dance to everyone you are playing this game with! Move on 2 spaces!

23

Make Some Noise!

Make Some Noise!

22

21

Make a trumpet noise, then move on 1 space.

Make Some Noise!

55

Throwing Shapes

The Trolls are throwing some awesome shapes on the dance floor!

Copy these dance shapes onto the grids opposite.

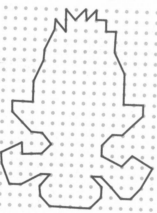
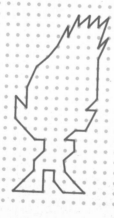

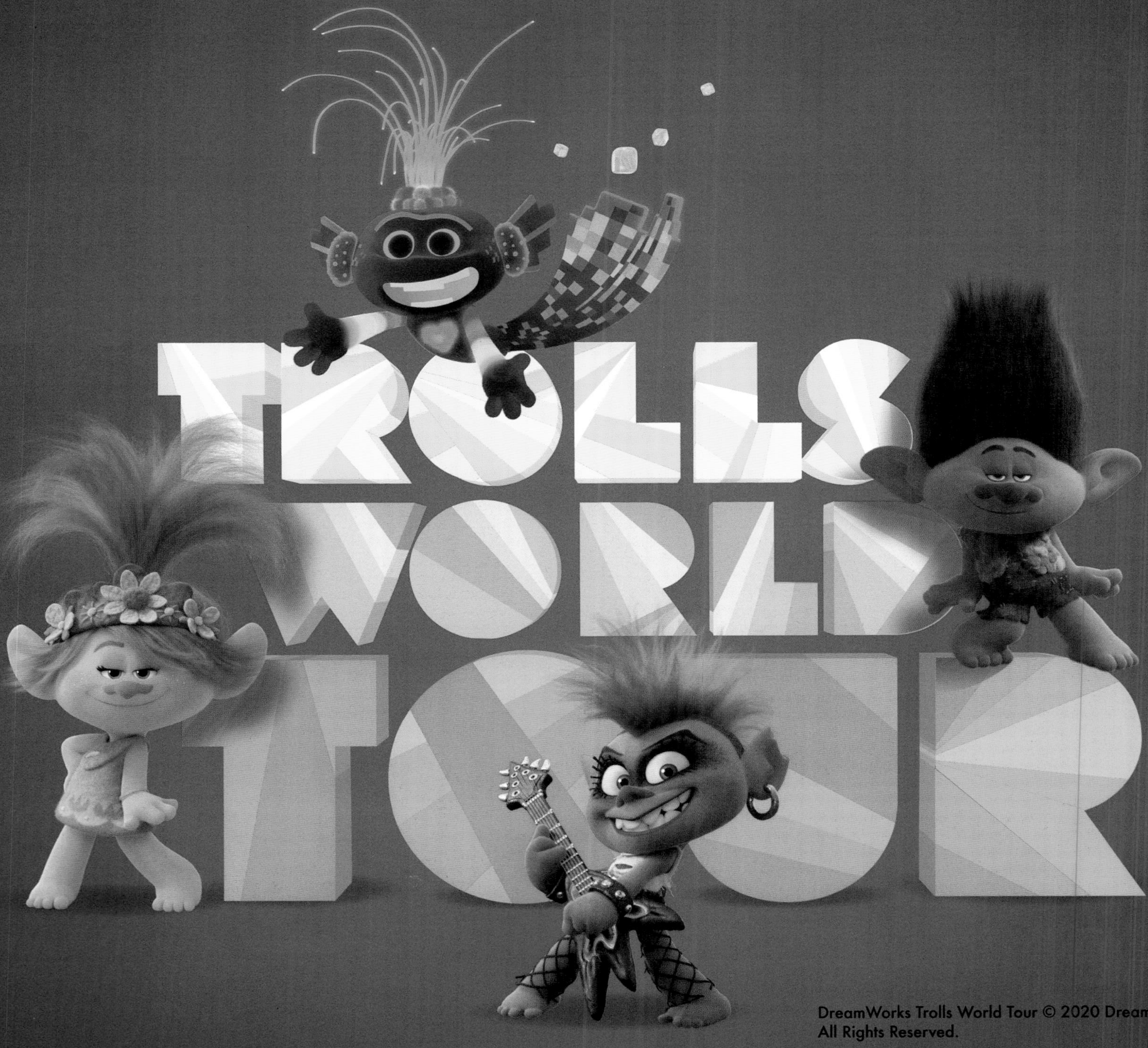
TROLLS WORLD TOUR

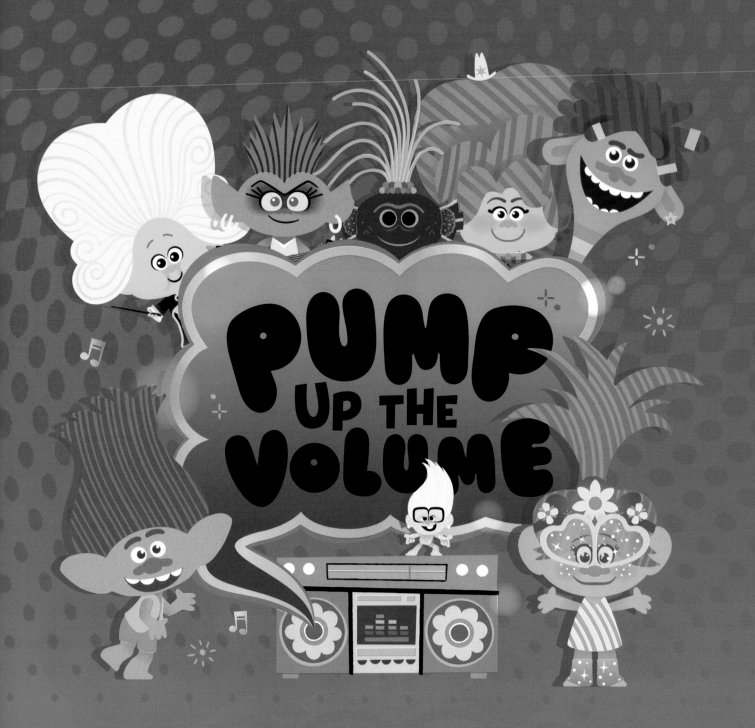

Coming Together

Poppy says that music comes from inside everyone and that we can all sing together in beautiful harmony. This pretty pattern shows all the different types of music in Trolls Kingdom, playing together as one.

Draw and colour in the missing half of the image to complete the beautiful harmony.

Story: Trolls World Tour

As Sheila B. flew, Poppy and Branch heard a noise. It was Biggie and Mr. Dinkles hidden under a tarp! They had fallen asleep eating treats!

"We're on a mission to help Barb unite the Trolls," Poppy explained.

"Let's land down there," said Poppy, spotting the smoking remains of a village.

"Hello?" said a high-pitched voice. **"Are you nice or mean?"**

"We're nice," said Poppy. **"What is this place?"**

"It was Symphonyville, where Classical Trolls lived," explained a little instrument named Pennywhistle. **"Then Queen Barb showed up with her Rock Army and blasted us with a rock guitar. She took**

our conductor, Trollzart, our string, our music and all the Classical Trolls!"

"Barb doesn't want to unite us," said Poppy. **"She wants to destroy us!"**

"We need to keep our string safe," said Branch.

"I am!" said Poppy, pulling the pop string out of her hair.

"Poppy, are you crazy?" shouted Branch.

"We have to stop Barb from destroying all music," said Poppy.

"How can we hug our way out of this one, Poppy?" said Biggie. Poppy pinky promised Biggie she would protect him no matter what!

"We'll ask the other Trolls to help us," said Poppy, looking at her map. **"The Country Western, Techno and Funk Trolls. We'll face Barb together."**

The Pop Trolls set off as determined Pennywhistle began rebuilding Symphonyville.

Cooper had also set off from Trolls Village on his very own adventure. Now he knew there were other Trolls out there, he was curious to find out if there were some like him. He loved Poppy and the other Pop Trolls a lot, but he'd always wondered why he looked a bit different from them

Meanwhile, Barb had the Techno and Classical Trolls strings.

"Only three more strings until we unite the world!" screeched Barb. **"And I'll play the ultimate power chord and unite the Trolls under one music. Rock!"**

Just then, Barb's bat delivered Poppy's reply:

Dear Barb,

Can't wait to meet you!
I have tons of great party ideas.
Maybe you and I can even be best friends!

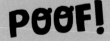

Glitter shot out of Poppy's card, sprayed
Barb in the face and pop music started playing!
Barb growled and started smashing up her tour bus!

61

The next morning, Poppy, Branch and Biggie reached Lonesome Flats, home of the Country Western Trolls. They listened as the mayor, Delta Dawn, sang a song.

"This song is so sad," said Poppy.

"Yeah," said Branch. **"But life is sad sometimes, so ... I kinda like it."**

To cheer them up, Poppy started singing cheerful pop music with Biggie. The Country Western Trolls didn't like it and started to get angry.

"That was a crime against music!" said Delta Dawn, putting Poppy, Branch, Biggie and Mr. Dinkles in jail!

"Wait no!" cried Poppy. **"We're here to warn you about Barb the Queen of Rock!"**

Suddenly there was a loud **TWANG**, as a lasso wrapped around the bars of the locked cell door and set them free. A Country Western Troll with a big white cowboy hat and four legs with hooves had come to save them!

"It ain't right to put you in jail just 'cause your music's different," he said. **"Name's Hickory! Hop on!"**

Branch was a bit wary of this stranger, but Poppy hopped on Hickory's back and they dragged the jail door with Biggie and Branch clinging on to it for dear life!

"Let's skedaddle!" shouted Hickory.

Delta Dawn spotted Hickory heading off with her prisoners and she and the other Country Western Trolls raced after them. **"CHARGE!"** she yelled.

Hickory and the Pop Trolls galloped off and down into a ravine. They managed to lose Delta and her gang. When they stopped to catch their breath, Branch whispered to Poppy that he was getting a weird vibe from Hickory and didn't trust him.

"But you don't trust anybody, Branch," whispered Poppy. **"The guy rescued us!"**

That night, as the Pop Trolls and Hickory sat by a fire, one of Queen Barb's bounty hunters called Chaz arrived. He played smooth jazz music that hypnotized Biggie, Mr. Dinkles, Branch and Poppy and trapped them in a cage.

"Soon, Queen Barb is going to have your string, and the world will be rid of pointless pop music once and for all!" gloated Chaz.

"Hold it right there!" said Hickory who had put gumdrops in his ears so he wasn't hypnotized. He pushed Chaz into the river and saved the Pop Trolls.

But Biggie was really upset. **"How are you supposed to save the world if you can't even keep us safe?"** he sobbed to Poppy. **"You made a pinky promise to protect us, Queen Poppy and you broke it."** And with that, Biggie headed back home with Mr. Dinkles.

Meanwhile, Cooper, who had taken himself on his own mission to find Trolls that were like him, was walking in the desert when ... **BOOM!** A bright light shone down and a bubble surrounded him! He was lifted up into the air and carried up into the observation room of a huge, shiny spaceship ...

The next day, Poppy was feeling sad about Biggie when she looked up. There was a spaceship right above her. It looked just like Vibe City on her map.

"I think we've found the Funk Trolls!" Poppy told Branch and Hickory.

Poppy got the spaceship's attention and bubbles were sent down to pick them all up! Then, **POP! POP! POP!** Their bubbles burst ...

"Welcome to Vibe City!"

"Cooper?" said Poppy surprised. **"What are you doing here?"**

"You mean what am I doing over here?" said a Troll from the other side of the room. **"Turns out I'm actually from Vibe City, just like my twin brother. Meet ... Prince D!"**

"What's poppin'?"
said Prince D.

Cooper then introduced Poppy to his mum and dad, King Quincy and Queen Essence. They thanked Poppy for looking after their long-lost son all these years ...

Suddenly loud sirens went off. The Rocker Trolls had arrived! Poppy told the Funk Trolls she could help, but they wanted to fight on their own. Branch agreed, but Poppy was upset.

The Funk Trolls sent Poppy and Branch safely back to land in bubbles. **"We always have different opinions,"** Branch said to Poppy. **"You and me are just too different."** And with that, he walked away and left Poppy to complete her mission without him.

Poppy chatted to Hickory about losing her friends. **"It's all because of this stupid string,"** she said, pulling it out.

"Run, Poppy!" said Hickory, as his two back legs started moving. Poppy watched as **ZIP!** a Troll called Dickory popped out the back. **"What are you doing, Hickory?"**

The two Trolls explained they were Yodelling Trolls disguised as one Country Western Troll the whole time!

"You were going to give Barb our string!" gasped Poppy.

"Yes, sorry," said Hickory. **"To save our yodelling."**

Just then, Queen Barb arrived. **"Nice job, fellas,"** she told the bounty hunters. She snatched the pop string.

"I'm not gonna let you do this!" cried Poppy.

Meanwhile, Biggie had made it home to Trolls Village and found that Barb had attacked it and taken nearly everyone to Volcano Rock City! The only ones left were Guy Diamond and Tiny Diamond, Legsly, Smidge, Satin and Chenille.

"Oh no!" said Biggie. **"I shouldn't have left Poppy. I've go to help her."**

"We're coming with you, Biggie!" said Legsly and the others.

And together, they came up with a plan ...

Volcano Rock City was where the Rocker Trolls played their super-loud concerts and where Barb was about to turn everyone into rock zombies.

Biggie, Legsly and the gang had disguised themselves as Rocker Trolls and were onstage as Barb's back-up band!

Riff shoved Poppy into a cage, while Barb attached the pop string to her guitar. The six strings glowed ...

"Who wants to see what the ultimate power chord can do?" roared Barb. But just as she did, Branch arrived. He'd come to save Poppy!

As Barb aimed her guitar at Poppy, Branch leapt in front and was instantly turned into a rock zombie!

Poppy picked the lock of her cell, but Barb turned her into a rocker too, and gave her the guitar.

The Pop Trolls looked horrified as Poppy began to play, but she winked at them. She didn't play rock, she played ...

"Pop music?" said Barb, confused.

Poppy pulled gumdrops out of her ears – she hadn't heard the rock power chord! She was saved! She broke the guitar strings and all the Trolls turned back to normal.

"Poppy's destroyed our music!" cried Barb.

The Trolls were silent, until, **THUMP-THUMP. THUMP-THUMP.** A beat! It was Cooper's heartbeat echoed with a microphone.

"Queen Barb can't take what's inside us," said Queen Essence. **"That's where music really comes from. Not strings."**

Poppy sang and all the Trolls joined in with their own styles. Even Barb!

Branch and Poppy realised they liked being different. They high-fived and made the perfect connection. **SMACK!**

Together the Trolls rebuilt their villages and learned that differences make us stronger!

THE END

The Ultimate Trolls World Tour Fan Quiz

Are you the ultimate Trolls World Tour fan?
Try these tricky true or false questions to find out!

1 Poppy and Branch are Pop Trolls.

TRUE/FALSE

2 The Pop Trolls are always singing Country Western music.

TRUE/FALSE

3 Tiny Diamond is Legsly's son.

TRUE/FALSE

4 Tiny Diamond likes to rap.

TRUE/FALSE

5 King Trollex is a DJ.

TRUE/FALSE

6 The Techno Trolls live up in the clouds.

TRUE/FALSE

7 Poppy headed off on her mission in Sheila B.'s basket.

TRUE/FALSE

8 Biggie and Mr. Dinkles were in Sheila B.'s basket.

TRUE/FALSE

9 The mayor of the Country Western Trolls sings happy pop songs.

TRUE/FALSE

10 Hickory is a Country Western Troll.

TRUE/FALSE

11 Cooper has a twin brother called Prince D.

TRUE/FALSE

12 Queen Barb wanted everyone to play rock music like her.

TRUE/FALSE

13 Riff is a Classical Troll.

TRUE/FALSE

14 This bat-like creature belongs to Barb.

TRUE/FALSE

15 Branch was turned into a rock zombie.

TRUE/FALSE

16 Poppy and Branch managed to high-five in the end.

TRUE/FALSE

Check your answers on page 69!

67

Answers

Page 8: Match the Moves

b is the matching shadow.

Page 9: Where's Mr. Dinkles?

c is the correct path.

Page 9: Rap it up!

My name is **Tiny Diamond**
And I glitter in the **sun**.
I hang out with troll **friends**,
And we have so much **fun**!
I love to sway to the hip hop **beat**
I dance and move and tap my **feet**!

Page 10: Escape from Bergen Town

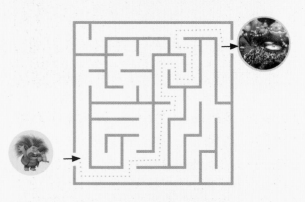

Page 11: Hobby Search

C	A	Y	T	C	H	D	W	A	C
G	L	T	S	O	G	B	E	E	M
C	R	O	C	H	E	T	I	N	G
R	F	E	M	G	P	W	G	A	N
E	O	B	G	C	A	A	H	Q	I
N	C	P	F	B	D	Y	T	C	G
A	U	C	Y	F	C	A	L	W	N
G	I	V	H	C	D	E	I	A	I
T	K	F	N	P	B	L	F	V	S
H	E	A	V	Y	M	E	T	A	L
M	U	G	R	I	S	K	I	B	D
B	C	T	A	A	O	A	N	D	A
D	R	D	H	R	I	F	G	C	A

Page 12: Whirling Word Wheel

BRANCH

Page 13: Spot the Difference

Page 18: Poppy's Flower Code

Now it's the hug time!

Page 19: Who's That?

a-Maddy; b-Fuzzbert; c-Smidge;
d-Cooper; e-Biggie; f-DJ Suki; g-Poppy;
h-Karma; i-Guy Diamond.

Page 23: Hug the Bug

6   7   3   2   1

Page 28: Fashion Fun

1

2

3

Page 29: Say cheese!

a-6; b-19; c-5; d-12; e-15; f-8; g-13; h-16; i-9; j-l; k-11; l-3; m-2; n-14; o-4; p-18; q-7; r-17; s-10.

Page 32: Question Time!

1. Branch
2. A pink microphone
3. In Biggies' hand
4. His left leg
5. Green
6. Green
7. Cooper
8. Heart shape
9. Pink
10. 11

Page 41: Techno Reef Maze

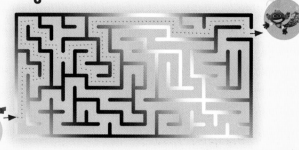

Page 42: Sudoku Symphony!

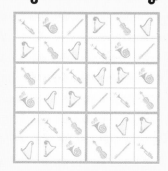

P43: Line Dance Line-Up

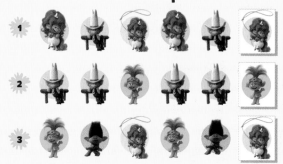

P44: Get Funky!

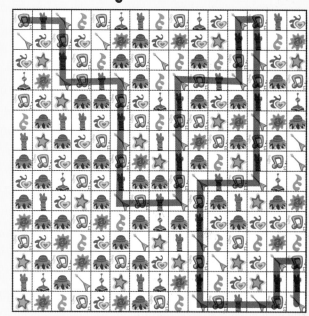

P45: Who Rocks?

Pages 66-67: The Ultimate Trolls World Tour Fan Quiz!

1. TRUE; 2. FALSE; 3. FALSE; 4. TRUE; 5. TRUE; 6. FALSE; 7. TRUE; 8. TRUE; 9. FALSE; 10. FALSE; 11. TRUE; 12. TRUE; 13. FALSE; 14. TRUE; 15. TRUE; 16. TRUE